# Dear Parents:

Congratulations! Your child is taking the first steps on an exciting journey. The destination? Independent reading!

**STEP INTO READING®** will help your child get there. The program offers five steps to reading success. Each step includes fun stories and colorful art or photographs. In addition to original fiction and books with favorite characters, there are Step into Reading Non-Fiction Readers, Phonics Readers and Boxed Sets, Sticker Readers, and Comic Readers—a complete literacy program with something to interest every child.

## Learning to Read, Step by Step!

### Ready to Read  Preschool–Kindergarten
• big type and easy words • rhyme and rhythm • picture clues
For children who know the alphabet and are eager to begin reading.

### Reading with Help  Preschool–Grade 1
• basic vocabulary • short sentences • simple stories
For children who recognize familiar words and sound out new words with help.

### Reading on Your Own  Grades 1–3
• engaging characters • easy-to-follow plots • popular topics
For children who are ready to read on their own.

### Reading Paragraphs  Grades 2–3
• challenging vocabulary • short paragraphs • exciting stories
For newly independent readers who read simple sentences with confidence.

### Ready for Chapters  Grades 2–4
• chapters • longer paragraphs • full-color art
For children who want to take the plunge into chapter books but still like colorful pictures.

**STEP INTO READING®** is designed to give every child a successful reading experience. The grade levels are only guides; children will progress through the steps at their own speed, developing confidence in their reading.

Remember, a lifetime love of reading starts with a single step!

Visit us on the Web!
StepIntoReading.com
randomhouse.com/kids

Educators and librarians, for a variety of teaching tools, visit us at RHTeachersLibrarians.com

ISBN 978-0-385-38462-9 (trade) — ISBN 978-0-388-53846-3 (lib. bdg.)

Printed in the United States of America

10 9 8 7 6 5 4 3 2 1

nickelodeon

DORA
and
Friends™

# MEET MY
# FRIENDS!

By Mary Tillworth

Illustrated by Dave Aikins

Random House New York

*¡Hola!* I'm Dora.

I live in a big city.

There is so much
to explore
in my new home!

Every day is
an adventure
with my new friends.
Come and meet them.

My friend Pablo
is so funny.
I laugh a lot
when I am with him.

Pablo loves to
explore with me.
We make
a great team!

Pablo solves problems.

Even by mistake!

My friend Emma

is a music star.

She plays

violin, guitar,

and piano.

Emma also gives
music lessons.

She is a
great teacher!

My friend Naiya
is very smart.
She loves
math and science.

She has her
own telescope
to look at the stars!

Naiya speaks
three languages.
And she wants
to learn more!

My friend Kate
loves stories.
She writes and acts
in her own plays!

Kate makes costumes
to wear onstage.
She loves
the spotlight!

My friend Alana
is good at sports.

She also loves animals.

She helps out

at the animal shelter!

My friends and I
try to help others
wherever we go.

Every day we try
to make our home
a better place!

I am so glad
you met my friends!
Now they are
your friends, too!